William Watson

The Father of the Forest

And Other Poems. Second Edition

William Watson

The Father of the Forest
And Other Poems. Second Edition

ISBN/EAN: 9783744711463

Printed in Europe, USA, Canada, Australia, Japan

Cover: Foto ©Andreas Hilbeck / pixelio.de

More available books at **www.hansebooks.com**

THE FATHER

OF THE FOREST

AND OTHER POEMS BY

WILLIAM WATSON

With Portrait after a Photograph
by Frederick Hollyer

LONDON : JOHN LANE, VIGO ST.
CHICAGO : STONE & KIMBALL
1895

Second Edition

Edinburgh: T. and A. CONSTABLE, Printers to Her Majesty

CONTENTS

THE FATHER OF THE FOREST

A

To John St. Loe Strachey

THE FATHER OF THE FOREST

I

OLD emperor Yew, fantastic sire,

   Girt with thy guard of dotard kings,—

What ages hast thou seen retire

   Into the dusk of alien things?

What mighty news hath stormed thy shade,

Of armies perished, realms unmade?

Already wast thou great and wise,

   And solemn with exceeding eld,

On that proud morn when England's eyes,

   Wet with tempestuous joy, beheld

Round her rough coasts the thundering main
Strewn with the ruined dream of Spain.

Hardly thou count'st them long ago,
   The warring faiths, the wavering land,
The sanguine sky's delirious glow,
   And Cranmer's scorched, uplifted hand.
Wailed not the woods their task of shame,
Doomed to provide the insensate flame?

Mourned not the rumouring winds, when she,
   The sweet queen of a tragic hour,
Crowned with her snow-white memory
   The crimson legend of the Tower?
Or when a thousand witcheries lay
Felled with one stroke, at Fotheringay?

THE FATHER OF THE FOREST

Ah, thou hast heard the iron tread
   And clang of many an armoured age,
And well recall'st the famous dead,
   Captains or counsellors brave or sage,
Kings that on kings their myriads hurled,
Ladies whose smile embroiled the world.

Rememberest thou the perfect knight,
   The soldier, courtier, bard in one,
Sidney, that pensive Hesper-light
   O'er Chivalry's departed sun?
Knew'st thou the virtue, sweetness, lore,
Whose nobly hapless name was More?

The roystering prince, that afterward
   Belied his madcap youth, and proved

A greatly simple warrior lord

    Such as our warrior fathers loved—

Lives he not still? for Shakespeare sings

The last of our adventurer kings.

His battles o'er, he takes his ease,

    Glory put by, and sceptred toil.

Round him the carven centuries

    Like forest branches arch and coil.

In that dim fane, he is not sure

Who lost or won at Azincour!

Roofed by the mother minster vast

    That guards Augustine's rugged throne,

The darling of a knightly Past

    Sleeps in his bed of sculptured stone,

And flings, o'er many a warlike tale,

The shadow of his dusky mail.

The monarch who, albeit his crown

   Graced an august and sapient head,

Rode roughshod to a stained renown

   O'er Wallace and Llewellyn dead,

And perished in the hostile land,

With restless heart and ruthless hand ;

Or that disastrous king on whom

   Fate, like a tempest, early fell,

And the dark secret of whose doom

   The Keep of Pomfret kept full well ;

Or him that with half careless words

On Becket drew the dastard swords ;

Or Eleanor's undaunted son,

    That, starred with idle glory, came

Bearing from leaguered Ascalon

    The barren splendour of his fame,

And, vanquished by an unknown bow,

Lies vainly great at Fontevraud ;

Or him, the footprints of whose power

    Made mightier whom he overthrew ;

A man built like a mountain-tower,

    A fortress of heroic thew ;

The Conqueror, in our soil who set

This stem of Kinghood flowering yet ;—

These, or the living fame of these,

    Perhaps thou minglest—who shall say ?—

THE FATHER OF THE FOREST

With thrice remoter memories,

    And phantoms of the mistier day,

Long ere the tanner's daughter's son

From Harold's hands this realm had won.

What years are thine, not mine to guess!

    The stars look youthful, thou being by ;

Youthful the sun's glad-heartedness ;

    Witless of time the unageing sky !

And these dim-groping roots around

So deep a human Past are wound,

That, musing in thy shade, for me

    The tidings scarce would strangely fall

Of fair-haired despots of the sea

    Scaling our eastern island-wall,

From their long ships of norland pine,

Their ' surf-deer,' driven o'er wilds of brine.

Nay, hid by thee from Summer's gaze

    That seeks in vain this couch of loam,

I should behold, without amaze,

    Camped on yon down the hosts of Rome,

Nor start though English woodlands heard

The selfsame mandatory word

As by the Cataracts of the Nile

    Marshalled the legions long ago,

Or where the lakes are one blue smile

    'Neath pageants of Helvetian snow,

Or 'mid the Syrian sands that lie

Sick of the day's great tearless eye,

Or on barbaric plains afar,

  Where, under Asia's fevering ray,

The long lines of imperial war

  O'er Tigris passed, and with dismay

In fanged and iron deserts found

Embattled Persia closing round,

And 'mid their eagles watched on high

  The vultures gathering for a feast,

Till, from the quivers of the sky,

  The gorgeous star-flight of the East

Flamed, and the bow of darkness bent

O'er Julian dying in his tent.

WAS it the wind befooling me

    With ancient echoes, as I lay?

Was it the antic fantasy

    Whose elvish mockeries cheat the day?

Surely a hollow murmur stole

From wizard bough and ghostly bole!

'Who prates to me of arms and kings,

    Here in these courts of old repose?

Thy babble is of transient things,

    Broils, and the dust of foolish blows.

12

Thy sounding annals are at best

The witness of a world's unrest.

'Goodly the ostents are to thee,

    And pomps of Time : to me more sweet

The vigils of Eternity,

    And Silence patient at my feet ;

And dreams beyond the deadening range

And dull monotonies of Change.

'Often an air comes idling by

    With news of cities and of men :

I hear a multitudinous sigh,

    And lapse into my soul again.

Shall her great noons and sunsets be

Blurred with thine infelicity ?

'Now from these veins the strength of old,

    The warmth and lust of life depart ;

Full of mortality, behold

    The cavern that was once my heart !

Me, with blind arm, in season due,

Let the aërial woodman hew.

'For not though mightiest mortals fall,

    The starry chariot hangs delayed.

His axle is uncooled, nor shall

    The thunder of His wheels be stayed.

A changeless pace His coursers keep,

And halt not at the wells of sleep.

'The South shall bless, the East shall blight,

    The red rose of the Dawn shall blow ;

The million-lilied stream of Night,

   Wide in ethereal meadows flow ;

And Autumn mourn ; and everything

   Dance to the wild pipe of the Spring.

'With oceans heedless round her feet,

   And the indifferent heavens above,

Earth shall the ancient tale repeat

   Of wars and tears, and death and love ;

And, wise from all the foolish Past,

Shall peradventure hail at last

'The advent of that morn divine

   When nations may as forests grow,

Wherein the oak hates not the pine,

   Nor beeches wish the cedars woe,

But all, in their unlikeness, blend

Confederate to one golden end—

'Beauty : the Vision whereunto,

   In joy, with pantings, from afar,

Through sound and odour, form and hue,

   And mind and clay, and worm and star—

Now touching goal, now backward hurled—

Toils the indomitable world.'

HYMN TO THE SEA

B

To Henry Norman

HYMN TO THE SEA

.

I

GRANT, O regal in bounty, a subtle and

delicate largess ;

Grant an ethereal alms, out of the wealth

of thy soul :

Suffer a tarrying minstrel, who finds, not

fashions his numbers,—

Who, from the commune of air, cages the

volatile song,—

Here to capture and prison some fugitive

breath of thy descant,

Thine and his own as thy roar lisped on

the lips of a shell,

Now while the vernal impulsion makes
lyrical all that hath language,
   While, through the veins of the Earth,
   riots the ichor of Spring,
While, with throes, with raptures, with
loosing of bonds, with unsealings,—
   Arrowy pangs of delight, piercing the
   core of the world,—
Tremors and coy unfoldings, reluctances,
sweet agitations,—
   Youth, irrepressibly fair, wakes like a
   wondering rose.

LOVER whose vehement kisses on lips
   irresponsive are squandered,
   Lover that wooest in vain Earth's imper-
   turbable heart;
Athlete mightily frustrate, who pittest thy
   thews against legions,
   Locked with fantastical hosts, bodiless
   arms of the sky;
Sea that breakest for ever, that breakest
   and never art broken,
   Like unto thine, from of old, springeth
   the spirit of man,—

21

Nature's wooer and fighter, whose years
are a suit and a wrestling,

All their hours, from his birth, hot with
desire and with fray ;

Amorist agonist man, that, immortally
pining and striving,

Snatches the glory of life only from love
and from war ;

Man that, rejoicing in conflict, like thee
when precipitate tempest,

Charge after thundering charge, clangs
on thy resonant mail,

Seemeth so easy to shatter, and proveth
so hard to be cloven ;

Man whom the gods, in his pain, curse
with a soul that endures ;

Man whose deeds, to the doer, come back as
thine own exhalations
Into thy bosom return, weepings of
mountain and vale ;
Man with the cosmic fortunes and starry
vicissitudes tangled,
Chained to the wheel of the world, blind
with the dust of its speed,
Even as thou, O giant, whom trailed in the
wake of her conquests
Night's sweet despot draws, bound to her
ivory car ;
Man with inviolate caverns, impregnable
holds in his nature,
Depths no storm can pierce, pierced with
a shaft of the sun ;

Man that is galled with his confines, and

burdened yet more with his vastness,

Born too great for his ends, never at peace

with his goal ;

Man whom Fate, his victor, magnanimous,

clement in triumph,

Holds as a captive king, mewed in a

palace divine :

Wide its leagues of pleasance, and ample

of purview its windows ;

Airily falls, in its courts, laughter of

fountains at play ;

Nought, when the harpers are harping,

untimely reminds him of durance ;

None, as he sits at the feast, whisper

Captivity's name ;

But, would he parley with Silence, with-

draw for awhile unattended,

Forth to the beckoning world 'scape for

an hour and be free,

Lo, his adventurous fancy coercing at once

and provoking,

Rise the unscalable walls, built with a

word at the prime ;

Lo, immobile as statues, with pitiless faces

of iron,

Armed at each obstinate gate, stand the

impassable guards.

III

MISER whose coffered recesses the spoils

of eternity cumber,

Spendthrift foaming thy soul wildly in

fury away,—

We, self-amorous mortals, our own multi-

tudinous image

Seeking in all we behold, seek it and find

it in thee :

Seek it and find it when o'er us the

exquisite fabric of Silence

Perilous-turreted hangs, trembles and

dulcetly falls ;

26

When the aërial armies engage amid
orgies of music,

Braying of arrogant brass, whimper of
querulous reeds ;

When, at his banquet, the Summer is
purple and drowsed with repletion ;

When, to his anchorite board, taciturn
Winter repairs ;

When by the tempest are scattered mag-
nificent ashes of Autumn ;

When, upon orchard and lane, breaks the
white foam of the Spring :

When, in extravagant revel, the Dawn, a
bacchante upleaping,

Spills, on the tresses of Night, vintages
golden and red ;

When, as a token at parting, munificent
Day, for remembrance,

  Gives, unto men that forget, Ophirs of
fabulous ore;

When, invincibly rushing, in luminous
palpitant deluge,

  Hot from the summits of Life, poured is
the lava of noon;

When, as yonder, thy mistress, at height of
her mutable glories,

  Wise from the magical East, comes like
a sorceress pale.

Ah, she comes, she arises,—impassive,
emotionless, bloodless,

  Wasted and ashen of cheek, zoning her
ruins with pearl.

Once she was warm, she was joyous, desire

    in her pulses abounding:

    Surely thou lovedst her well, then, in her

    conquering youth!

Surely not all unimpassioned, at sound of

    thy rough serenading,

    She, from the balconied night, unto her

    melodist leaned,—

Leaned unto thee, her bondsman, who

    keepest to-day her commandments,

    All for the sake of old love, dead at thy

    heart though it lie.

IV

YEA, it is we, light perverts, that waver, and

   shift our allegiance ;

   We, whom insurgence of blood dooms to

   be barren and waste ;

We, unto Nature imputing our frailties, our

   fever and tumult ;

   We, that with dust of our strife sully the

   hue of her peace.

Thou, with punctual service, fulfillest thy

   task, being constant ;

   Thine but to ponder the Law, labour and

   greatly obey :

50

Wherefore, with leapings of spirit, thou
chantest the chant of the faithful,
Chantest aloud at thy toil, cleansing the
Earth of her stain ;
Leagued in antiphonal chorus with stars
and the populous Systems,
Following these as their feet dance to the
rhyme of the Suns ;
Thou thyself but a billow, a ripple, a drop
of that Ocean,
Which, labyrinthine of arm, folding us
meshed in its coil,
Shall, as now, with elations, august exulta-
tions and ardours,
Pour, in unfaltering tide, all its unani-
mous waves,

When, from this threshold of being, these

steps of the Presence, this precinct,

Into the matrix of Life darkly divinely

resumed,

Man and his littleness perish, erased like

an error and cancelled,

Man and his greatness survive, lost in

the greatness of God.

THE TOMB OF BURNS

C

To the Hon. Mrs. Henniker

THE TOMB OF BURNS

WHAT woos the world to yonder shrine?

What sacred clay, what dust divine?

Was this some Master faultless-fine,

  In whom we praise

The cunning of the jewelled line

  And carven phrase?

A searcher of our source and goal,

A reader of God's secret scroll?

A Shakespeare, flashing o'er the whole

  Of man's domain

The splendour of his cloudless soul

And perfect brain?

Some Keats, to Grecian gods allied,

Clasping all Beauty as his bride?

Some Shelley, soaring dim-descried

Above Time's throng,

And heavenward hurling wild and wide

His spear of song?

A lonely Wordsworth, from the crowd

Half hid in light, half veiled in cloud?

A sphere-born Milton cold and proud,

In hallowing dews

Dipt, and with gorgeous ritual vowed

Unto the Muse?

Nay, none of these,—and little skilled

On heavenly heights to sing and build !

Thine, thine, O Earth, whose fields he tilled,

And thine alone,

Was he whose fiery heart lies stilled

'Neath yonder stone.

He came when poets had forgot

How rich and strange the human lot ;

How warm the tints of Life ; how hot

Are Love and Hate ;

And what makes Truth divine, and what

Makes Manhood great.

A ghostly troop, in pale amaze

They melted 'neath that living gaze,—

His in whose spirit's gusty blaze

We seem to hear

The crackling of their phantom bays

Sapless and sear!

For, 'mid an age of dust and dearth,

Once more had bloomed immortal worth.

There, in the strong, splenetic North,

The Spring began.

A mighty mother had brought forth

A mighty man.

No mystic torch through Time he bore,

No virgin veil from Life he tore;

His soul no bright insignia wore

Of starry birth;

He saw what all men see—no more—

In heaven and earth :

But as, when thunder crashes nigh,

All darkness opes one flaming eye,

And the world leaps against the sky,—

So fiery-clear

Did the old truths that we pass by

To him appear.

How could he 'scape the doom of such

As feel the airiest phantom-touch

Keenlier than others feel the clutch

Of iron powers,—

Who die of having lived so much

In their large hours ?

He erred, he sinned : and if there be

Who, from his hapless frailties free,

Rich in the poorer virtues, see

His faults alone,—

To such, O Lord of Charity,

Be mercy shown !

Singly he faced the bigot brood,

The meanly wise, the feebly good ;

He pelted them with pearl, with mud ;

He fought them well,—

But ah, the stupid million stood,

And he—he fell !

All bright and glorious at the start,

'Twas his ignobly to depart,

Slain by his own too affluent heart,

Too generous blood;

And blindly, having lost Life's chart,

To meet Death's flood.

So closes the fantastic fray,

The duel of the spirit and clay!

So come bewildering disarray

And blurring gloom,

The irremediable day

And final doom.

So passes, all confusedly

As lights that hurry, shapes that flee

About some brink we dimly see,

The trivial, great,

Squalid, majestic tragedy

Of human fate.

Not ours to gauge the more or less,

The will's defect, the blood's excess,

The earthy humours that oppress

The radiant mind.

His greatness, not his littleness,

Concerns mankind.

A dreamer of the common dreams,

A fisher in familiar streams,

He chased the transitory gleams

That all pursue ;

But on his lips the eternal themes

Again were new.

With shattering ire or withering mirth

He smote each worthless claim to worth.

The barren fig-tree cumbering Earth

    He would not spare.

Through ancient lies of proudest birth

    He drove his share.

To him the Powers that formed him brave,

Yet weak to breast the fatal wave,

A mighty gift of Hatred gave,—

    A gift above

All other gifts benefic, save

    The gift of Love.

He saw 'tis meet that Man possess

The will to curse as well as bless,

To pity—and be pitiless,

    To make, and mar ;

The fierceness that from tenderness

    Is never far.

And so his fierce and tender strain

Lives, and his idlest words remain

To flout oblivion, that in vain

    Strives to destroy

One lightest record of his pain

    Or of his joy.

And though thrice statelier names decay,

His own can wither not away

While plighted lass and lad shall stray

    Among the broom,

Where evening touches glen and brae

With rosy gloom ;

While Hope and Love with Youth abide ;

While Age sits at the ingleside ;

While yet there have not wholly died

The heroic fires,

The patriot passion, and the pride

In noble sires ;

While, with the conquering Saxon breed

Whose fair estate of speech and deed

Heritors north and south of Tweed

Alike may claim,

The dimly mingled Celtic seed

Flowers like a flamc ;

While nations see in holy trance

That vision of the world's advance

Which glorified his countenance

　　When from afar

He hailed the Hope that shot o'er France

　　Its crimson star;

While, plumed for flight, the Soul deplores

The cage that foils the wing that soars;

And while, through adamantine doors,

　　In dreams flung wide,

We hear resound, on mortal shores,

　　The immortal tide.

SONNETS

I THINK you never were of earthly frame,

O truant from some charméd world
unknown!

A fairy empress, you forsook your
throne,

Fled your inviolate court, and hither
came;

Donned mortal vesture; wore a woman's
name;

Like a mere woman, loved; and so are
grown

At last a little human, save alone

For the wild elvish heart not Love could
tame.

D

And one day I believe you will return

To your far isle amid the enchanted sea,—

There, in your realm, perhaps remember

me,

Perhaps forget: but I shall never learn!

I, loveless dust within a dreamless urn,

Dead to your beauty's immortality.

TO ———

IF, on these pale and trembling blooms, full
  soon   .
The winter of oblivion should descend,
Remember, it was in my summer's noon
  I gave you the poor posy, gentle friend.
Remember, how a fickle gust of praise
  Ruffled my foliage in that perished time,
And by the after-light of these dead days
  Read once again my world-forgotten
  rhyme.

Say : 'Fame his mistress was ; he wooed
   her long,
   She toyed with him an hour—and flung
   him by :
With me alone the memory of his song
   Reluctant fades, and hesitates to die.'—
Then burn the book, that eyes less kind
   than those
Vex not the haunted dusk of its repose.

THE TURK IN ARMENIA

WHAT profits it, O England, to prevail

In camp and mart and council, and
bestrew

With sovereign argosies the subject
blue,

And wrest thy tribute from each golden
gale,

If, in thy strongholds, thou canst hear the
wail

Of maidens martyred by the turbaned
crew

Whose tenderest mercy was the sword
that slew,

And lift no hand to wield the purging flail?

We deemed of old thou held'st a charge
from Him

Who watches girdled by His seraphim,

To smite the wronger with thy destined
rod.

Wait'st thou His sign? Enough, the sleep-
less cry

Of virgin souls for vengeance, and on high

The gathering blackness of the frown of
God!

March 2nd, 1895.

LYRICS

I DO not ask to have my fill

Of wine, or love, or fame.

I do not, for a little ill,

Against the gods exclaim.

One boon, of Fortune I implore,

With one petition kneel :

At least caress me not, before

Thou break me on thy wheel.

OH, like a queen's her happy tread,
And like a queen's her golden head!
But oh, at last, when all is said,
    Her woman's heart for me!

We wandered where the river gleamed
'Neath oaks that mused and pines that
    dreamed.
A wild thing of the woods she seemed,
    So proud, and pure, and free!

All heaven drew nigh to hear her sing,
When from her lips her soul took wing;
The oaks forgot their pondering,
    The pines their reverie.

And oh, her happy queenly tread,

And oh, her queenly golden head!

But oh, her heart, when all is said,

Her woman's heart for me!

APOLOGIA

APOLOGIA

THUS much I know: what dues soe'er be

    mine,

Of fame or of oblivion, Time the just,

Punctiliously assessing, shall award.

This have I doubted never; this is sure.

But one meanwhile shall chide me,—one

    shall curl

Superior lips,—because my handiwork,

The issue of my solitary toil,

The harvest of my spirit, even these

My numbers, are not something, good or ill,

63

Other than I have ever striven, in years

Lit by a conscious and a patient aim,

With hopes and with despairs, to fashion
    them ;

Or, it may be, because I have full oft

In singers' selves found me a theme of
    song,

Holding these also to be very part

Of Nature's greatness, and accounting not

Their descants least heroical of deeds ;

Or, yet again, because I bring nought
    new,

Save as each noontide or each Spring is
    new,

Into an old and iterative world,

And can but proffer unto whoso will

A cool and nowise turbid cup, from wells

Our fathers digged ; and have not thought

    it shame

To tread in nobler footprints than mine

    own,

And travel by the light of purer eyes.

Ev'n such offences am I charged withal,

Till, breaking silence, I am moved to cry,

What would ye, then, my masters ? Is the

    Muse

Fall'n to a thing of Mode, that must each

    year

Supplant her derelict self of yester-year ?

Or do the mighty voices of old days

At last so tedious grow, that one whose lips

Inherit some far echo of their tones—

APOLOGIA

How far, how faint, none better knows than
    he
Who hath been nourished on their utter-
    ance—can
But irk the ears of such as care no more
The accent of dead greatness to recall?
If, with an ape's ambition, I rehearse
Their gestures, trick me in their stolen
    robes,
The sorry mime of their nobility,
Dishonouring whom I vainly emulate,
The poor imposture soon shall shrink
    revealed
In the ill grace with which their gems be-
    star
An abject brow; but if I be indeed

Their true descendant, as the veriest hind

May yet be sprung of kings, their linea-
  ments

Will out, the signature of ancestry

Leap unobscured, and somewhat of them-
  selves

In me, their lowly scion, live once more.

With grateful, not vain-glorious joy, I
  dreamed

It did so live; and ev'n such pride was
  mine

As is next neighbour to humility.

For he that claims high lineage yet may feel

How thinned in the transmission is become

The ancient blood he boasts; how slight
  he stands

In the great shade of his majestic sires.

But it was mine endeavour so to sing

As if these lofty ones a moment stooped

From their still spheres, and undisdainful
graced

My note with audience, nor incurious heard

Whether, degenerate irredeemably,

The faltering minstrel shamed his starry
kin.

And though I be to these but as a knoll

About the feet of the high mountains,
scarce

Remarked at all save when a valley cloud

Holds the high mountains hidden, and the
knoll

Against the cloud shows briefly eminent;

APOLOGIA

Yet ev'n as they, I too, with constant
    heart,

And with no light or careless ministry,

Have served what seemed the Voice ; and
    unprofane,

Have dedicated to melodious ends

All of myself that least ignoble was.

For though of faulty and of erring walk,

I have not suffered aught in me of frail

To blur my song ; I have not paid the
    world

The evil and the insolent courtesy

Of offering it my baseness for a gift.

And unto such as think all Art is cold,

All music unimpassioned, if it breathe

An ardour not of Eros' lips, and glow

With fire not caught from Aphrodite's
    breast,

Be it enough to say, that in Man's life

Is room for great emotions unbegot

Of dalliance and embracement, unbegot

Ev'n of the purer nuptials of the soul ;

And one not pale of blood, to human
    touch

Not tardily responsive, yet may know

A deeper transport and a mightier thrill

Than comes of commerce with mortality,

When, rapt from all relation with his kind,

All temporal and immediate circumstance,

In silence, in the visionary mood

That, flashing light on the dark deep,
    perceives

Order beyond this coil and errancy,

Isled from the fretful hour he stands alone

And hears the eternal movement, and
  beholds

Above him and around and at his feet,

In million-billowed consentaneousness,

The flowing, flowing, flowing of the world.

Such moments, are they not the peaks of
  life?

Enough for me, if on these pages fall

The shadow of the summits, and an air

Not dim from human hearth-fires some-
  times blow.

www.ingramcontent.com/pod-product-compliance
Lightning Source LLC
Chambersburg PA
CBHW030020030726
47499CB00008B/3062